When hope see

Never
Too Late

Danielle
Knight

Grey Cat
Press

Never Too Late
Copyright 2013 © Danielle Knight
Published by Grey Cat Press

First Edition

This is a work of fiction. Names, characters, places,
and incidents are either the product of the author's
imagination or are used ficticiously and are not to be
construed as real. Any resemblance to actual events,
locales, organizations, or persons, living or dead, is
entirely coincidental.

Image: Male Model
copyright: Andrei Vishnyakov | Dreamstime.com
Image: Silhouette of Romantic Couple Sitting on a Beach
copyright: Igor Stepovik | Dreamstime.com
Please note that the man in the image is a model who is
in no way to be connected with the character in this book.

ISBN-13: 978-1483966144
ISBN-10: 1483966143

Grey Cat Press

For more information about any book published by
Grey Cat Press, please visit www.greycatpress.com

*This one is dedicated
to all the dreamers
on all the beaches
throughout the world...*

When hope seems lost, the heart knows best...

Never Too Late

Danielle Knight

One

Patricia Ann Foster bit back a tired sigh. With a quiet thump, the remnants of her suitcase pushed through a dark curtain in the wall and dropped down onto the conveyor that ran the length of the Marathon Field baggage claim area. It sat on its back, broken and abused. A clear plastic garbage bag was stuffed inside, held there by a few strands of duct tape. The bag contained what had once been a carefully-packed wardrobe, the assortment of hair-care and skin products necessary to survive a week on a remote island, and the very expensive and not yet worn underwear that she'd purchased as a reward for working during what would have been—

for anyone else—a relaxing getaway to one of the most romantic beaches in the Florida Keys...

But not her.

Never her.

Tall, dark, and handsome was a dream, just like fairytale castles and happily ever afters. For Patricia Ann Foster, the time for dreaming had long since come and gone.

Taking a deep breath, Patti went to her happy place. It was a familiar trip. Anymore, she seemed to end up there several times every day.

In the eternity from one heartbeat and the next, Patti reminded herself—rather pointedly—that she could handle the crisis of the approaching piece of shattered luggage. It wasn't really a crisis, in fact. She'd been planning for it since the moment she learned that the old miser refused to spring for the cost of a direct flight. It might have been nice to be *wrong,* for a change—and to be pleasantly surprised for once in her life—but with three stopovers and four airlines in the ten-hour trip from Boston to the Keys, the battered suitcase had been doomed from the start.

Fortunately, she'd packed a few essentials inside her carry-on bag, like the floral skirt, the red tank top, and the flat sandals that she'd changed into after departing an airplane that was barely the size of a commuter van... along with her purse, a phone, her laptop, and the paperback novel that she'd been hoping to read on the beach.

From deep inside her happy place, she continued to watch the suitcase rumble and bump its way toward her on a dirty strip of rubber that hadn't been cleaned since the last century.

That was when she noticed the note.

It sat in the bag, a white stamp of doom sandwiched tightly between the bulging plastic and a wadded-up suit jacket that was dry-clean only. She recognized the letterhead from clear across the room. With all the traveling she did for her cheapskate boss, she'd seen it dozens of times before. The bag had been *randomly selected* for screening by some jack-booted security-agency thug who obviously hadn't liked what he'd seen, or who, perhaps, liked what he'd seen just a little too much. Between brain-dead baggage handlers and the smirking security agents, the suitcase hadn't stood a prayer.

Why did she even bother?

Patti exhaled her frustrations and dark thoughts through tight lips, letting them lift a travel-ravaged auburn curl from her forehead as they drifted through the heavy, flower-scented air over the heads of the dozen other passengers—couples, mostly—who rushed to claim their undamaged bags and begin their romantic adventures beyond the rectangle of warm sunlight in the far wall beyond a double row of dusty leather lobby chairs. She'd soon be joining them, in spirit if not in body. In another hour or so, she'd be enjoying a cold beer or a glass of white wine at the bungalow—she hadn't quite decided which—followed by a slow walk on the beach with the sand in her toes, the breeze in her hair, and a blazing sunset low on the horizon.

With her book, of course... and absolutely alone.

Patti hadn't *planned* for the job to take over her life. She'd just sort of looked up one day and suddenly noticed how much time had passed. How many long years. How many lost sunsets. How many empty beaches...

It just sort of happened.

The worst is over, she reminded herself, snapping her attention back to the task at hand. It was far too late to look back at what might have been. Best just to rise above it and move on.

Patti could repair the damage to her wardrobe, even if the tightwad would never let it fly on her expense report. Shady Palm Key might have been the most secluded and romantic vacation spot in the Keys, as well as home to the insolvent insurance company that the Commissioner hired her boss to investigate, but with a hundred-mile highway plowing right through the middle it was far from a desert island. She could surely find a dry cleaners and a department store *somewhere*.

Leaving the happy couples to carry on with their romantic vacations, Patti settled the strap of her carry-on bag firmly over her shoulder—the only *carrying on* that she ever did—and headed to the carousel to retrieve the last disaster that she would allow to intrude upon her trip.

The worst was over, she reminded herself again. There was nothing but clear sailing ahead.

She refused to let it be any other way.

Two

Kirk Carter sat in a wicker chair on the back veranda of the two-bedroom beach bungalow that his client asked him to use for the week. Fine. Twist his arm. Bare feet on the railing and cold beer in hand, he watched the last fingers of sunlight begin to fade from a shining sky that was getting ready to sprout a million bright little stars. A gentle sea breeze was blowing in; not much, but enough to rustle the palm fronds overhead and escort the last of the daily heat away from the hardwood deck beneath the chair that he'd pushed back on two legs. The tang carried the rich smell of flowers, a smell that perfume companies spent billions trying to imitate—most of them very badly.

It was set to be a glorious night.

The perfect end to a glorious day.

Not every Friday did Kirk have the chance to swim the warm, turquoise waters of the Florida Keys, or to relax in nothing but a beach towel while watching a spectacular sunset after showering away the salt. Cold beer and sunsets. There was something to be said for the island style. Even a boy who grew up in the bustling city could see that.

Kirk had to hand it to the old man. The beach bungalow had a certain flair, a certain class. Sparse by design, the sunken floor of the central living room held a surprisingly comfortable green leather couch with a mahogany frame and carved wooden posts. The matching green leather armchairs that flanked it were equally comfortable, and the ornate mahogany coffee table in the center of the room—along with the rough granite lamps burning low against the coming night from the sturdy end tables—gave it that masculine man-cave feel while still letting everyone inside gaze through the glass wall at a magnificent westward view... something most man caves simply did not do. But then, guys weren't supposed to appreciate things like sunsets.

Watch a sunset?

Don't be daft!

Where was the wide-screen television?

Where were the football games?

The identical bedrooms in the satellites off to either side of the living room were equally masculine and equally tasteful, with heavy beds, bulky nightstands, solid lamps, and equally impressive views... which was how Kirk knew that Brian Orson couldn't possibly own the place. The little weasel didn't have a tasteful bone in his entire body.

Orson *had* talked someone else out of the pad for the week, however, and talking someone out of such a gem was still a pretty impressive feat. If it was Kirk's place, he'd never let anyone as shady as Brian Orson near it, much less any of Orson's associates.

Kirk raised his bottle to the old man's spunk. Not everyone could swing the sweet deals he'd managed, either with the bungalow's owner or with the Insurance Commissioner. Kirk had no problem taking a piece of Orson's action... provided he received a healthy retainer up front, and also provided that the balance of the bill was paid on time...

Kirk still couldn't figure Orson's angle.

Why had the little guy tossed in free room and board for the assignment? Kirk wasn't looking a gift horse in the mouth, or anything. The money he saved would be better spent after-hours at the local night clubs, anyway. It might have been true that Shady Palm Key didn't have an abundance of those—based on the scouting he'd done that afternoon—but surely he could find something on one of the neighboring keys. One of these days, he might even get lucky and find the future Mrs. Right... but not if he didn't get out there and mingle. The right gal wouldn't just fall into his lap from the clear blue sky.

Kirk was still admiring the last of the sunset, enjoying the last of his beer, and trying to finalize his plans for the first weekend of his working vacation when a crash at the front door snapped his head around. The chair spun on its back leg. Off balance, Kirk toppled over his shoulder and slammed down hard with his feet flying up in the air.

"Son of a... sugar biscuit!" he barked, rubbing the back of his head. Rolling onto his knees, he pushed himself to his feet, then blinked hard to make sure his eyes were working once he finally looked though the glass wall to see what, or more specifically *who,* had made the racket that dumped him from his chair.

"Oh, no!" he said, shaking his head. "Hell no! That's not happening. No way!"

Beyond the sunken living room, a woman lay sprawled across a shattered suitcase on the landing at the front door next to his kitchen alcove. From beneath a tangle of auburn curls, she lifted her head to stare at him, round-faced and with big green eyes: Patti Foster... the biggest wet blanket on the planet.

This was not happening!

The old man had set him up, but good.

Patti was five or six years older than Kirk and a genuine pain in the ass—a prude who wore her hair pulled back into a braid so tight and so severe that it tugged all the fun from her face, her life, and anyone else who happened to be stuck in the same room with her. Kirk had worked with her on some of the old man's contracts in the past. Those few brief hours had been the absolute longest eternities of his entire damned life.

Kirk continued to rant through the glass, his arms waving in the cool evening air. With his mouth on autopilot and his mind shifting into overdrive, he would never remember his exact words, but even with his brain busy figuring the angles and trying to decide exactly what the old man had in mind, one thought gradually began to intrude: there was something different about Patti, something he couldn't quite pinpoint.

The big green eyes that continued to stare up at him from across the room, all *deer-in-the-headlights,* were softer than they should have been, for one thing. Hell, the whole *package* was softer than it should have been. It wasn't just the eyes though, which were surprisingly large. It wasn't just the hair, either, which was surprisingly long and curly—a deeper shade than he'd remembered... and with fine streaks of red and gold mixed in for good measure. And it wasn't... well...

It just wasn't any *one* thing.

He'd never seen Patti in anything but a power suit before. Maybe that was it. Power suits did not do her justice.

Patti had a compact figure with an amazing set of hips that she showed to great effect beneath a light floral skirt. She also had a modest but impressive endowment that played hide-and-seek from within the slightly large tank top that rested snugly against the curves on her right, while dropping down—loose and baggy and quite suggestively—to her left. It was a surprisingly fun outfit, and that surprisingly-fun outfit begged an even bigger question...

Exactly *when* had Patti Foster learned to have fun?

The question stirred other thoughts, as well—thoughts that finally allowed a second realization to grab the spotlight, a realization that possibly explained why the woman continued to lay sprawled across her suitcase while staring up at him from across the room...

It was starting to get *very* drafty.

Kirk's mouth froze mid-rant. He glanced down.

His beach towel sat wadded up and tangled in the overturned chair at his feet.

Three

Willpower could move mountains. No one knew that better than Patricia Ann Foster. Her life had been one mountain-moving exercise after another. Hell, she'd moved entire *ranges* of mountains with her willpower before, but even that indomitable will was powerless in the face of a tight-fisted boss determined to make her trip to paradise a living hell.

After collecting her belongings at the baggage carousel, Patti had gone looking for the car that she'd been promised would be waiting for her out at the curb.

She'd found it...

A beat-up two-door Buick.

He hadn't even sprung for a town car.

The driver—a dark-skinned man with bad teeth, a wide smile, gray hair, and a scruffy growth of whiskers on his chin—might have spoken English, but he did so with an accent so lazy and so carefree that the words flowed together in one unending, incomprehensible stream of sound that more resembled a musical river than any reasonable attempt at speech. After wrestling her own bag into the trunk—and nearly ripping her hem on a jagged piece of metal while repeatedly slamming the lid—she'd tried to climb into the back seat from the passenger side, only to have the man reach over to open the door from the inside, since neither of the handles apparently worked from the outside.

The first thing she smelled after settling into the car—aside from the stench of stale cigarettes—was the grease. Her eyes had gone momentarily round as she slid her hand roughly against the chapped leather beside her and checked her palm to see if her white floral-print skirt would have a black backside when she left the car.

She'd been relieved to see a clean hand. Unfortunately, her moment of relief evaporated as the car sped away from the curb. Her driver's attention to detail while driving was exactly as precise as his attention to detail while speaking.

Her white-knuckled, meandering trip down a nearly endless series of bridges and roads—during which the man used nearly as much pavement on the left side of the line as the right—came to an end several lifetimes later just as the gold fire of the setting sun was fading from the fronds over a scattered cluster of beachside bungalows nestled beneath a stand of palm trees.

She'd wasted the entire day traveling.

So much for her walk on the beach.

So much for her good book.

Patti had been nervous when her driver turned off the highway and headed down an isolated dirt road that shouldered its way through the palm trees toward the beach, but now that she was here and starting to notice the exotic cars with their immaculate paint jobs parked around the other bungalows scattered throughout the trees, she grew even more nervous, but for an entirely *different* reason.

Her tightwad boss promised that she'd have complete run of the place. He'd promised that there'd be a car at the house that she could use. This was not a cheap beachfront bungalow, however, and these were definitely not the types of cars that just anyone could borrow.

"There must be some mistake."

"No mee-stake," the man said, taking her bag from the trunk and waving to the bungalow with a toothy smile. Another sing-song string of sentences began to flow from his mouth. She couldn't understand the words, but the carefree confidence was clearly evident. He hopped back into the car and drove away before she could argue, leaving her standing at the doorstep with the hope that his carefree confidence was justified.

She'd found the key where he promised, though, which was a good sign... but then she discovered that the front door was unlocked, which was not.

The doorknob turned easily.

The heavy wooden door swung free.

"Hello?" she called out, knocking as she lugged her suitcase inside and set it on the landing, then leaned on the handle. "Is anyone here?"

That was when she saw him... the man, the stranger—a dark silhouette framed by a sky that was still bright from the setting sun. He sat in a chair on the veranda outside her living room, his muscular shoulders practically glowing in the light. He seemed huge, a giant. For one brief moment, she wondered what it might feel like to run her fingers over those broad shoulders, or to be wrapped up in those powerful arms...

Then she grew nervous again for the *first* reason. A man like that, anything could happen.

And then something *did* happen—

The handle of her battered suitcase broke. Patti tumbled over the top, crashing to the floor. A moment later, an answering crash vibrated through her palms. She looked up from beneath a wild tangle of disarrayed auburn curls to see the giant of a man pick himself up from the overturned chair on the deck.

He faced her, then gestured sharply to indicate he was speaking. She couldn't hear a word he said through the glass, but she immediately noticed that his shoulders weren't the only things that were bare. Backlit by the setting sun, his silhouette might not have revealed much—aside from the outline of his powerful shoulders, his narrow waist, and a set of rock-hard thighs—but she couldn't force herself to look away.

The kindling warmth at the pit of her stomach matched the heat in her cheeks. As she lay there, sprawled out over her broken suitcase, that kindling warmth flashed upward to touch her trembling heart and downward to fire emotions that would have been best left alone—especially at a romantic beachside bungalow, and most especially in the presence of a stranger.

Then the man noticed his problem.

Bending, he grabbed a towel from his feet and wrapped it around his waist, cinching it tight. A moment later, he righted the chair and opened a sliding glass door.

"What the hell are you doing here?" he demanded while still outside.

She'd expected the question. What she didn't expect, however, was the sound of the voice.

Her brow dropped.

A frown tugged the corner of her mouth. She knew the sound of that voice, but from where?

He stepped inside the lighted room.

"Kirk!" she practically spat, scrambling to her feet. The sudden heat cooled almost as quickly as it had come. "I'm supposed to be here. What the hell are *you* doing here?"

Kirk Carter.

She couldn't believe it.

Kirk was an insufferable little prick—or maybe not quite so *little,* as her slowing heart was quick to point out, but no matter. He was arrogant and rude, a playboy with absolutely no work ethic who occasionally happened to get lucky and make enough wild guesses in his reports to fool her tightwad boss into thinking that he actually knew his stuff. The fact that he also *knew,* beyond the shadow of a doubt, that he was God's gift to women always made Patti want to lose her lunch. She'd worked with Kirk before. She swore that each never-ending eternity would be her last. Unfortunately, she never had the final say in such matters.

"Great," he snapped, turning to close the door, but when he turned to face her again, his angry frown was gone. "Looks like we've been set up," he added with a slightly resigned and rueful shake of his head. "Now I get it. You know, I gotta hand it to the guy. Orson's gonna pick up a few thousand bucks right here. Two consultants; two bedrooms. He doesn't need to reimburse our hotel rooms, but he can turn right around and charge the client for the use of an extravagant little cottage that's not even his. He's always got an angle."

"I am *not* an angle," Patti snapped, still hot.

"No, you're not," he said simply, his blue eyes sincere. "Nice hair, by the way. I don't think I've ever seen you wearing it down before. It looks good on you."

Had *Kirk Carter* just paid her a compliment?

Patti fought the urge to touch her hair as she watched him standing in his towel, his thick black hair flopped so arrogantly across his forehead, his blue eyes glittering with mischief and his cocky smile showing how much he appreciated Orson's little joke. She refused to notice the way his broad shoulders leaned up against the glass with his biceps crossed at his chest, too; or his long, lean torso and the way the light from the hard granite lamps played so softly across the ridges and valleys of his tight abs.

She would *never* notice such things.

Not in such an insufferable prick.

"Of course, we might have problems at tax time," he mused, pushing off the glass and strolling to the couch in the center of the room with complete disregard for the fact that he was half naked and there was a lady in the room. Turning, he dropped down with his back to her, giving an excellent view of his neck and shoulders—not that she noticed. "Trouble is," he added, "when we pay for a room and get reimbursed for it, it's a wash on our books. Cash in, cash out. No tax event, right? But when we're given a room to use, sometimes we need to claim the value. It's the same as cash coming in the door, per the IRS. Orson wouldn't even think about that. Trouble is, we don't have an off-setting expense. No cash going back out. Sometimes, the imputed value is taxable. You might want to check with your accountant."

"Imputed value? That's ridiculous," she said, still standing in the entryway.

"To you and me, but not to the IRS. If you don't like it, fire your congressman.

He's the moron who made the law. Better check with your accountant, like I said. You gonna stand there all night, or are you coming in?"

"I don't know," she said, dragging the suitcase to the edge of the sunken living room. "Are you going to sit there in your towel all night, or are you putting on some clothes?"

"Towel covers more than my swim trucks," he replied with a shrug, his muscle bunching and then relaxing from the action. "Besides, you've already seen everything there is to see."

"Not that I'd have even been interested in trying, but in case you hadn't noticed, the sun is setting. You were in full silhouette, genius. I didn't see a thing."

"You didn't... I mean... oh," he stammered, some of the swagger leaving his voice as he stared straight ahead, his neck beginning to heat. Had it all been an act? Had he tossed around that bit of bravado just to hide the fact that God's

gift to women was actually *embarrassed?*
"That's good. I mean, I wouldn't want to spoil the show."

"Which show is that?"

"You know," he shrugged again. "When we go walking on the beach."

"Who said anything about a beach? We're here to work, Mister Carter—"

"The job doesn't start until Monday, Miss Foster. We've got the whole weekend ahead of us—"

"And far too many reports to review in just two days."

This time he did turn his head.

"Reports?" he asked, genuinely puzzled. "What reports?"

"The company financials—"

"The financials! Why would we ever want to review those?"

"Mister Orson asked me to review all of the financial statements prior to our arrival. He always does. That's the way we do business. We want to hit the ground running."

"He pays you for that?"

"He pays me for the job. I get a flat fee, same as you."

Kirk opened his mouth with a quick reply, but then clicked it shut. When he opened it again, his words were slow and measured—not quite condescending, but infuriatingly quiet, as if speaking to a child.

"Patti, the company is insolvent. The reports were lies. You're on a tropical beach. You've got two whole days away from the winter weather up north. Why would you waste any of that time studying a bunch of lies?"

"Because that's what some of us do," she told him. "It's called a work ethic. You should try it sometime."

"My work ethic's just fine, thank you," he said, turning back to finish watching his sunset. "Thing is, Patti, you gotta take the time to enjoy the moments. They don't come with trumpets or fanfares. They just sort of sneak up on you and then try to slip past. You don't want to wake up one day and find that they're all gone."

"My moments are just fine, thank you," she replied, a twist of his own words. "Speaking of moments, I still have things to do with mine. Two bedrooms, you said. Which way's mine?"

He pointed right without looking up. She turned and began dragging her suitcase down the hall on its rumbling wheels. As she left the room, she might have heard him mutter something under his breath. It was faint and not meant for her ears, but over the noise of the wheels he might have said, "Guess I was right, all along."

Four

The next morning, Kirk busied himself over breakfast in the kitchen alcove. It wasn't much of a kitchen, but then, he wasn't much of a cook.

A small refrigerator, a dishwasher, and a sink ran along the outer wall behind him, with a microwave on the counter beneath the overhead cabinets in the corner. The refrigerator was large enough to handle the case of beer he'd bought—once the bottles were stacked on their sides—but it had trouble with the height of the milk carton and the width of the egg container; the dishwasher was perfect for a bachelor, but it would never handle an entire day for a family of four; and the sink was barely wide enough to wash the plates.

Kirk leaned back against the dishwasher in his board shorts and a yellow tee-shirt. The fork that he held absently in his right hand mixed a double batch of milk and eggs in a small bowl in his left as he looked out the window. The kitchen was only as wide as the stove against the wall to his left. His bare toes were butted up against the inner half-wall, the kitchen's only redeeming feature—an imitation granite slab that doubled as extra counter space from his side, and a dining room table from the other.

It might not have been much of a kitchen, but it had one heck of a view.

Through the living room and beyond the deck, the cobalt waters that stretched off toward a distant island were framed by stands of palm trees and a sandy white beach that practically begged for company. Kirk could still feel the crunch of the cold sand beneath his toes from the midnight stroll he'd taken to clear his head. He'd thought the palm-scented air and a moonlit beach might do the trick. He'd been wrong.

Until yesterday, Patti Foster hadn't been a mystery. She'd been a zero. She was a mousy bookworm, and *not* in the sexy-librarian kind of way. She was the kind of person who wanted to be left alone—the kind of person who'd bite your head off if you forgot yourself and opened a door for her, or if you ever made the mistake of greeting her with a cheerful *good morning.* She was the kind of person you did your business with and then left alone...

Or so he'd thought.

Before yesterday, he'd ignored the quiet voice at the back of his mind that told him he was wrong. Life was too short to waste time puzzling out a prude, even if his eyes kept tracking back to her whenever she was in the room. He'd told himself it was because she was such a pain in the ass, but perhaps he'd been wrong about that, too.

He'd spent a sleepless night in that cold, hard bed until the vision that appeared every time he closed his eyes finally drove him outside—the vision of

Patti Foster sprawled over her luggage in the entryway and staring up at him from across the room.

At first, he'd convinced himself it was the suggestive pose, something worthy of any men's magazine: the flare of her amazing hips in that skimpy skirt... the cling of her tank top against those impressive curves... the arch of her spine... some other bit of macho bullshit.

But it wasn't any of that.

It was her eyes.

Her eyes had driven him outside.

For the brief moment that she hadn't known who he was, those expressive green eyes shined with raw emotions that he would never have thought to see—hope and fear and mystery and longing, plus dozens of others that flashed too fast for him to catch. For that brief moment, her eyes hadn't been the cold, hard things he was used to seeing. They'd been the kind of eyes that made the quiet voice at the back of his mind nod in smug satisfaction... the kind of eyes a guy could spend a lifetime exploring...

But he was talking about *Patti*.

A rustling from down the hall and the soft patter of feet snapped Kirk's attention back to the eggs. The gurgling coffee pot at the side of the granite slab filled the room with the sharp smell of French Roast, and the softly-humming toaster next to it added the scent of warming bread to the air, but the blob of half-melted butter in the skillet suggested quite strongly that breakfast was going to be a runny disaster if he couldn't coax a little more heat from the stove.

"Morning," he said, risking her wrath with half of a full *'good morning'* when her dark shape finally rounded the corner to block the light at the corner of his eye as he used the fork to zip the butter around the skillet to make it melt faster.

"Is that coffee I smell?" she asked in reply, pulling the middle of three stools from beneath the counter and sliding up onto the seat.

"Freshly made," he said, pouring the eggs into the skillet and hoping for the best. "The mug next to it is yours, if you'd like. I didn't think to buy sugar. Need milk?"

"No, black's fine."

She reached for the pot while he rested the fork on the lip of the skillet—tongs down in the eggs—then poured herself a mug as he dropped the empty bowl into the sink and filled it with water. Shutting off the faucet, he turned around with a forced smile on his face, fully prepared to engage in the mindless small talk that people used to fill up the empty spaces of their morning—

And tried not to stare.

Patti sat with her elbows on the counter and her head tilted down as she sipped at the mug that she held in both hands. The soft autumn curls of her sleep-tangled hair spilled down across the shoulders of a green silk robe that perfectly matched the shade of her eyes. It was belted loosely at the front and fell forward against her arms, revealing the pale green fabric of a wispy sleep shirt trimmed in lace—a shirt that was so wispy, in fact, that it drooped forward along with her robe to offer an erotic hint of the pale curves and dusky valley barely concealed within.

She looked up, her eyes big and round and sprinkled with flecks of gold that he'd never noticed. Strange. He hadn't noticed the brace of freckles splashed across the crescents of her cheeks, either—

"What, I got dirt on my face?"

"Um... I mean.. no," he stammered. Fortunately, the toaster saved him from any further reply. Two barely-browned slices of bread sprang up with a loud *ka-chang*. They wouldn't have been nearly toasted enough on any other day, but today their timing was perfect. "Plates. Where do we keep the plates?" he asked, turning to reach up into the cupboard high overhead.

Why was he being such a pinhead? It wasn't like he'd never seen a woman before. Hell, he'd been married to one for three years, even if that had been many, many moons ago. In all that time, though, she'd never once slept in a wispy little night shirt, or even cared to own a silk robe. She'd told him that sexy things like that were gimmicks cooked up by ad executives to meet their monthly sales quotas. She'd opted to sleep in one of his old shirts, instead; and her bathrobe was big and fuzzy, not at all sexy, with a matching set of slippers...

But Patti had come alone.

She'd expected to *be* alone.

This was how she normally slept.

Amazing.

"Thanks," she said when he returned with the plates. "Toast is fine."

"What? No eggs? I made 'em special."

"No. Thanks. A bagel and a coffee is all I ever have. You sleep well?" she asked, changing subjects as he moved the small tub of butter and the butter knife from the side of the stove to the counter where she could reach it.

"Like a rock, " he lied. "You?"

"Same here," she lied right back. She hadn't slept like a rock. She'd been studying those damned reports until well past two, not that he'd been checking.

He'd opened his window with the slim hope that the gentle song of the nearly-calm ocean waves might lull him to sleep. He'd seen the light spilling out onto the deck. It was hard to hide the glow of a bedside lamp on such a dark island.

"Good. You're gonna need it. We got a lot of exploring to do."

"Excuse me?" she blinked.

"The Keys," he said. "We've got a car, a gorgeous day, *lots* of sunshine, and a whole boatload of tourist traps to explore."

Snorting, she shook her head. "The only thing I need to explore is a dry cleaners. I've got too much work to finish before the end of the day. I can't waste any time."

"The assignment doesn't start until Monday," he reminded her. "Besides, I think I already mentioned that reading those lies is the true waste."

"Not to Mister Orson," she countered. "He's waiting on my analysis. He's already called once this morning to find out how I'm doing."

"He called *here* at nine o'clock on a Saturday morning? Why didn't I hear the phone?"

"Probably because you were still asleep. It was seven-thirty."

"I guess that explains it," he said, but not for the reason she thought. He'd been outside again after watching a dazzling sunrise during another extended walk to clear his head. Shady Palm Key wasn't the biggest island in the world. Before the week was up, he suspected he'd be memorizing every foot of its five-mile beachfront.

"I guess it does," she started to say, but the cascading chimes of an incoming phone call interrupted her thought. For a moment, Kirk couldn't believe what he'd heard.

"You carry your phone in your *bathrobe?*"

"Don't you?" she asked, hopping off the stool and retrieving the phone. "Yes?" she said, turning her back and crossing the living room. "Yes, Mister Orson. I'm still looking at the numbers...

no, I haven't found anything yet... Huh? What's that?"

Kirk would never know what the two of them might be discussing. Before the one-sided conversation could go any further, she stepped through the sliding glass door and closed it behind her.

Kirk shook his head.

Orson was a real ass.

Patti was a consultant, the same as Kirk. She'd let it slip that Orson talked her into a flat rate for the contract. Every other consultant on the planet was hourly. She'd be lucky to get a third of what she was worth, or even a quarter. The man had also convinced her to work an extra weekend to perform the due diligence work that he should have already done, himself. It was enough to make Kirk's blood boil.

He tried to tell himself that his feelings had nothing to do with the way the ocean breeze played with the hem of a very short and very sexy green silk robe outside the window, or the way the lace trimmed fabric of a set of wispy shorts that matched a wispy pale-green top played a little too much in the breeze to reveal just a little too much of the soft, lower curve of a certain someone's shapely caboose...

Caboose?

Where the hell had *that* come from? Why was he suddenly having a hard time thinking of it as an ass, even to himself? What's more, why was he even *thinking* about Patti's ass, or about the way those smooth curves might feel while cuddled up and playing spoons in a soft bed, or even the most burning question of all: whether or not she had a set of cute little dimples just beneath the small of her back?

Kirk was still honest enough with himself to know that before yesterday, he wouldn't have cared about any of it. He wouldn't have thought twice about calling it an ass, he wouldn't have wondered what she'd feel like folded up in his arms, and he certainly wouldn't have worried about the fact that she was getting screwed... but that still didn't mean that he knew what to do about it.

A growing sizzle and the smell of burning eggs snapped his eyes to the skillet.

Leaping left, he snatched the fork and hastily attacked the eggs. Breaking up the brown skin at the bottom, he scrambled the soft pieces into the unburned mixture up top as he shut down the burner and let the skillet's heat finish the job.

It was just as well that Patti hadn't wanted any eggs. His first breakfast in the small alcove at Shady Palm Key did not promise to be his finest. After a long night of thinking and a morning filled with even more questions, there was only one thing Kirk knew for an absolute truth...

It wasn't much of a kitchen, but that was okay. He wasn't much of a cook, either.

Five

Patricia Ann Foster hadn't had the best of mornings. She hadn't slept well in the cold, hard bed at Shady Palm Key—not just because she'd been reviewing reports until nearly three in the morning, and not just because the ocean and the inviting white sand beach were calling to her from just beyond her closed window, and certainly not just because the matching set of naughty new underwear that she'd bought as a reward for this stupid assignment was the one thing that hadn't managed to make the trip. No, Patricia Ann Foster hadn't had the best of mornings because she hadn't been able to shake the image of that maddening man's shoulders, or the way his silhouette stood out so trim and hard against the sunset when she'd first arrived.

The afternoon started no better.

After replacing her cold piece of toast with one fresh from the toaster when she'd finally managed to get off the phone—and then taking the cold one for himself—the maddening man had suggested quite calmly, through a perfect smile, with his bright blue eyes sparkling beneath a tangled shock of thick dark hair, that they drive to one of the neighboring keys to take care of her little wardrobe emergency. He'd even checked already and found a place with two-hour service.

Where was the self-absorbed asshole? What had this imposter done with the one arrogant little snot on the entire planet that Patti Foster absolutely could not stand? Why did her eyes keep lingering over the casual curve of the shoulders that were barely concealed within that yellow tee-shirt, and when would her thoughts quit wandering back to the chiseled thighs that were now entirely hidden by that ghastly set of straight-cut board shorts?

How was any of this possible?

"Another hour," Kirk said from the other side of the patio table after checking a wristwatch that he'd donned specifically for the occasion. She'd opted for a pale yellow strapless sundress and flat sandals for their brief outing, but in addition to the wristwatch, he'd only added a pair of white sneakers—sans socks. "How are you holding out? Need another?"

"I'm fine," she said, glancing at the Bloody Mary in front of her. She'd almost ordered a Virgin Mary, but she'd changed her mind when she'd caught him trying to keep from rolling his eyes as she placed the order. He'd been right, of course. One drink was *not* going to kill her. More importantly, she could now pretend that the fire building down below was due to the alcohol, even if that didn't explain why her fingers itched to brush away the errant lock of hair that kept falling across his forehead in the gentle breeze.

"Yes, you are," he chuckled, flashing her a cocky grin that did more than the vodka to warm her heart, "but that wasn't the question. Sing out if you'd like something more. It's never too late to change your mind."

Something more.

She wanted something more, all right; and that was the problem. It was *years* too late for the fleeting thoughts dancing through her mind. Happily ever after only happened in stories. Too bad, too. Away from the office, he seemed to be a real Prince Charming...

There had to be a catch.

After escorting her to his car—*escorting* her to his car—which was a basic Chevy four-door rental, rather than something exotic like she'd first feared, he'd taken her on a scenic drive through the bright sunshine and the warm tropical air to a larger key twenty miles away.

How he'd managed to make a scenic drive of a trip across a highway that hopped directly from one key to the next was anyone's guess, but by the time they arrived she'd felt like they'd wasted a deliciously sinful amount of time... or, perhaps that was simply the voice at the back of her mind that nagged about all the paperwork she had yet to plow through.

Whatever.

They'd dropped her dry cleaning off and paid for the two-hour rush, then found a beachside restaurant a few blocks away that just happened to be entertaining Happy Hour for lunchtime on that particular day... and every other day of the week, for that matter.

Kirk steered them to one of the dozen round glass tables scattered throughout the patio—the one with the best view of the beach over a low patio wall—then held out the chair facing the ocean and helped her into her seat before hustling around to the other side and sitting down with his back to the surf.

With the sun warming her bare shoulders and the vodka giving her a slight buzz, Patti began to relax for the first time since she'd arrived. Reluctantly, she had to admit the value of Kirk's hair-brained plan. Perhaps she didn't need to work the *entire* weekend, after all.

"Speaking of changing your mind, you mentioned something about taking a flat fee for the job," he said, lifting his own Bloody Mary to his lips. "Ever think of going hourly?"

Where had that come from?

Why did he suddenly want to talk about the job after spiriting her away from her work?

"Mister Orson has always only offered a flat fee," she said. "I mean, I asked him about it in the beginning, but he assured me that was how it was done. He refused to budge."

His eyes, which had been bathing her in their warmth all morning, flicked off to her right. When he spoke again, his words seemed hesitant, almost distracted.

"You've gone a few miles since then. It might be too late to change this job, but it's never too late to look ahead. You're a contractor... your own company. You've got to value your time, right? If you don't do it, who will?"

Valuing her time was never an issue. Paying the bills was the issue. With the government taking a healthy share, and her health care taking another, it seemed that the more she made, the less able she was to squeak by.

"As you say, I'm my own company, but he's my only client. If I insult him, I won't get any more jobs. That's not very good for the bottom line."

Taking a healthy drink, he set his glass back onto the table.

"Oh, I don't know. Seems to me a bit of honest negotiating never hurt anyone. You might think about it for the next time. You never know until you try."

The words seemed sincere, but for some reason he was finding it very hard to meet her eyes. He continued to smile and look across the table, but his eyes kept flicking to her right. He'd been so warm and calm and supremely confident before they'd sat down. Was it something she'd done, or was all the sudden talk about changing her mind really a code for trying to break it to her that he was changing *his* mind?

"Negotiating?   I don't understand. The negotiating's done," she shrugged, quietly glancing to her right... and then the storm clouds gathered as she discovered the reason for his distraction.

She was tall and blonde, with perfect hair and perfect teeth. She sat by herself at a table against the side of the building in a skimpy pink string bikini with a short, matching wrap and enough artificial enhancements to cause a worldwide plastic shortage. It was a wonder that she could even walk.

"Each job is different," she suddenly realized he'd been saying.   "If you're not too obvious about it, you can often negotiate a better deal each time around."

Not too obvious about it?

A better deal?

Patti was quickly starting to realize that there was a bit of subtle negotiating going on beneath her very eyes.   The blonde was a home wrecker. Patti could practically see the notches on her garter belt; but Kirk was obviously interested, and from the looks the bimbo was tossing back, his little friend was definitely just as interested in returning his attentions.

She should have known better.

Hell, she *had* known better.

Why hadn't she listened?

She'd been right about Kirk, all along.

"Oh, I get it. Negotiation," she snapped, suddenly furious at herself and trying very hard not to dash her drink at him across the table. "Is that what's going on here? Is that why your little friend is suddenly so interested?"

"My what?" he asked a little too sharply, caught in the act.

"You're little friend," she replied. "I've got eyes, you know."

She had his full attention now. He stared at her, his blue eyes round in mock confusion and his mouth opening and closing like a fish out of water. It made her all the more angry.

How dare he even *pretend* that she hadn't noticed!

He really *was* an insensitive prick.

"Tell you what," she said, rising from the chair with fury flashing up her neck. "I wouldn't want to come between the two of you. I'd rather wait at the cleaners. By all means, take your time. I'm sure you can find a quiet corner to finish your... negotiations... without me. I'll meet you in the car in an hour."

"What the hell is *that* supposed to mean?" he finally blurted.

"Don't even pretend that I don't know!" she snapped, spinning on a heel and storming away. She swept past the quietly-smirking blonde without glancing down, although she did break her promise to herself and look back right before ducking around the corner.

Everything was as she'd thought.

Kirk continued to stare after her in mock confusion, but the bimbo was already rising from her table and moving across the patio to take Patti's spot.

Six

"...speaking of changing your mind, you mentioned something about taking a flat fee for the job," Kirk told Patti, sliding into a conversation that he'd repeatedly told himself to ignore. "Ever think of going hourly?"

He looked across the table with a smile in his eyes. It was hard to tell whether or not she had a smile in hers. He'd left his sunglasses in the car so she could see his eyes. He'd wanted to lessen the risk of any misunderstandings, but she was still wearing hers—big and black and a little on the intimidating side, especially when a person was easing into a difficult conversation.

"Mister Orson has always only offered a flat fee," she said. "I mean, I asked him about it in the beginning, but he assured me that was how it was done. He refused to budge."

Kirk almost snorted. The old man was a real bastard. He'd snowed her good, burying her so deep in his flat-fee bullshit that it might take hours of gentle persuasion to dig her back out.

He tried to focus on the task at hand, but the sun and those damnable shades made it hard—the sun because it shined so bright in her auburn hair, bringing out those incredibly soft golden highlights, and the shades because he couldn't look at them for long without dropping his eyes... and what he found waiting for him when he did *that* was an even bigger distraction.

"You've gone a few miles since then," he told her reasonably with a slight shrug. "It might be too late to change this job, but it's never too late to look ahead. You're a contractor... your own company. You've got to value your time, right? If you don't do it, who will?"

She nodded as if in understanding, but then offered him one of her own shrugs and said, "As you say, I'm my own company, but he's my only client. If I insult him, I won't get any more jobs. That's not very good for the bottom line."

The shrug was a bad idea.

That dress was *very* distracting.

Strapless was fine, so was playful and carefree. He liked playful. He liked carefree. He liked the fact that the mousy little bookworm prude had turned into a surprisingly sexy butterfly, even if it had taken him forever to notice; but the tight bodice from her tiny waist to just beneath her bust made everything above it look so damned much bigger...

Or maybe not.

How would he know?

More to the point, why should he even wonder if she really was that big, and why had he never noticed before? Was his sudden interest real, or was it just something in the water? It sure seemed real, but he'd heard about people getting carried away during vacations only to find that things weren't the same when they got back home.

"Oh, I don't know," he said, trying to find a safe place for his eyes and settling for the shadows next to the building over her right shoulder. "Seems to me a bit of honest negotiating never hurt anyone. You might think about it for the next time. You never know until you try."

"Negotiating? I don't understand. The negotiating's done," she shrugged again, with the same results.

The bounce tugged his eyes back down to the table. He quickly snapped them up and into those dark sunglasses to see if she'd noticed—which she probably had—before sending them back to the safety of the shadows... after they dropped back down on their own accord for one more parting glance.

What the hell was wrong with him? It was just a damned shrug—carefree like the dress. The breasts resting so comfortably atop that tight lower bodice rocked gently within the folds of that softly-gathered material, though, and that carefree action tried its best to sidetrack a very serious conversation that he probably shouldn't have been discussing with her, anyway.

Breasts.

Had he actually started thinking of them as breasts? And when had he started noticing hers? Tits, cans, jugs, melons... ass. Maybe ass wasn't such a bad word for something so wonderful, after all. God! She was driving him nuts! She was driving the little guy nuts, too... or was Kirk doing that to himself by trying so damned hard not to think about all the wonderfully soft curves hiding a mere arm's length away beneath a light and carefree pale yellow sundress?

She was an older woman. They were both past their prime. They weren't a couple of giddy kids out on a prom date. They'd worked together many times without a second thought. What the hell was going on?

"Each job is different," he suggested gently, ripping his mind back to the task at hand. She was incredibly sweet and incredibly bright—not to mention incredibly sexy—and the old man was taking incredible advantage of her on every single job. If nothing else, Kirk was going to convince her to never again charge a flat fee for her services if it was the last thing he did! "If you're not too obvious about it, you can often negotiate a better deal each time around."

"Oh, I get it," she suddenly said, interrupting his train of thought. "Negotiation. Is that what's going on here? Is that why your little friend is suddenly so interested?"

"My what?" he asked, trying to keep his voice far more calm than it suddenly felt. He'd been trying to be a little more discrete. Sure, she'd been driving the little guy nuts, but that was hardly his fault. It was her own fault for being so damned sexy.

And how had she managed to see beneath the table, anyway? He'd been blessing the God of Baggy Board Shorts that he'd accidentally stumbled into the perfect attire for the morning's outing.

Even if she'd peeked beneath the table, how had she managed to notice enough of the little guy to be offended by his reaction in the first place?

"You're little friend," she repeated. "I've got eyes, you know."

Apparently so... X-ray vision, in fact.

"Tell you what," she said, suddenly very angry and rising like a titan from her chair, "I wouldn't want to come between the two of you. I'd rather wait at the cleaners. By all means, take your time. I'm sure you can find a quiet corner to finish your negotiations without me. I'll meet you in the car in an hour."

"What the hell is that supposed to mean?" he blurted.

Wasn't she maybe overreacting just a little? It wasn't like he'd propositioned her, after all. She was the one who'd brought it up! And what did she expect him to do, anyway... find that quiet little corner she mentioned and service the problem, himself?

"Don't even pretend that I don't know!" she snapped, storming away.

What the hell did *that* mean?

"Women," he muttered, staring at her as she stomped off. Totally confused, he kicked himself for being such a fool as to bring up such a sensitive subject on what had promised to be such a gorgeous day. He was still staring after her when a woman's voice drifted down over the black rain cloud that seemed to come from nowhere to blot out the sun.

"Is this seat taken?"

"Huh?" he asked, looking up.

He stared up into a ghastly wooden face that had been ruined by far too much plastic surgery and a cold, hard chest that went beyond the ridiculous. The fashion magazines might disagree, but Kirk never found the fad of puffing up a woman's lips to be the least bit appealing, and to erase all the graceful lines of her natural wrinkles was a crime. There was beauty in all things, particularly women. Kirk was a huge fan of *natural*, regardless of what a woman's natural state happened to be. Nothing that man touched could ever compare.

"The chair?" the blonde in the pink bikini repeated, gesturing to Patti's empty seat.

"Oh, um... no," he said, rising and walking around the table to help her into the chair. After scooting it in to the table, he added, "Help yourself. Enjoy. I was just leaving."

With a polite smile, he turned and moved across the patio, gliding through the sun with a purposeful stride. He didn't know precisely what he'd said to ruin the day, but he *did* know that it was never too late to fix a mistake. Nothing worth saving was worth throwing away. The last twenty-four hours had surprised Kirk by showing him that Patti well might turn out to be one of the most worthwhile things in his life, but not if he didn't fix things.

He had the glimmer of a screwy idea.

It wasn't much, but perhaps it just might be enough.

Either way, he only had fifty-nine minutes to work it all out.

Seven

Patti steamed on the couch, staring blankly at the financial report in her lap.

It was her own damned fault.

For a moment—for a single *moment*—she'd relaxed her guard and started thinking that perhaps there was something remotely human about the arrogant, self-centered little prick that she happened to be sharing a beachside bungalow with in the middle of a tropical paradise so lovely that she could never have envisioned it in a million lifetimes. She'd let the possibilities of the exotic location tempt her with feelings best forgotten and blind her to the hard reality of the one true lesson that thirty-plus-plus years had drummed into her life—even if, after all these years, she still insisted to anyone who asked that she wasn't a day over twenty-nine. That one true lesson was this: men were jerks.

So, okay, keeping her mouth shut during the long ride back from town might have been the hardest thing she'd done in her life, and keeping her eyes from straying to the muscles bunched up in the calves of his stubby legs and the chiseled thighs that peeked out from beneath his board shorts might have been a close second—although that task grew much easier when she realized she could still see the reflections in the passenger window if she kept her head turned away from him at all times—but those were natural reactions. Animal reactions. Animal *magnetism.*

Lust.

There was a huge difference between love and lust. Every woman on the planet knew that, even if men did not. For Patricia Ann Foster, the time for love had long since come and gone. For one very brief moment, she'd forgotten it was far too late for fairytale endings. She'd let lust rule the day, masquerading as love to rip her heart out when she'd been hit with the cold, hard truth.

"It's your own damned fault," she muttered, just as it was her own damned fault that she was now beginning to wonder if she'd overreacted.

For one brief moment that morning, the alcohol had finally started to relax her to the point where she'd honestly wondered if maybe she should throw caution to the wind and do something incredibly satisfying and equally stupid. Lust might not be love, but it had been so very long, and who knew if—or *when*— the chance might come again.

Kirk warned her to enjoy the moments. She'd laughed it off, but now she was wondering if that moment might have, indeed, been... well... no matter. Now, she'd never know. She'd almost been willing—almost—but he'd thrown it all away over a bimbo.

Patti's eyes snapped up to the window when she heard the first heavy footfalls rumble from the stairs that were out of sight at the side of the porch. Kirk was coming back from the second walk he'd taken that afternoon. With the sun just starting to drop low enough on the horizon to fill the glass wall and flood the living room in an orange light that would soon grow uncomfortably bright, even Patti had to reluctantly admit that it was a nice enough day for it.

Warm air, white-sand beaches, gentle surf, turquoise waters...

A stack of financial reports.

The footsteps reached the top of the stairs. Patti's eyes snapped down. A moment later, a shadow crossed the artificial rose that sat in a crystal bud vase in the middle of the grossly-ornate coffee table. The sliding glass door *whooshed* open. The sounds of the beach entered the room as Kirk poked his head inside.

"You done with that? Come on. The sun's great. How 'bout a walk on the beach? I found this great little cove on the other side of the key. Crystal clear water, almost emerald green. The only trouble is that when the locals are there, they don't bother with swimsuits. You might need to cover your eyes. What do you say?"

"No."

"No what? No, you're not done? No, you don't want to go for a walk? No, you'd rather not cover your eyes?"

"No," she repeated without looking up.

"Party pooper," he muttered, stepping inside. The door whooshed shut behind him. Slipping out of his sneakers, he crossed the living room on bare feet and asked, "So, what's got you so interested in those reports, anyway? I didn't see anything but a cartload of horse pucky."

She had no intention of answering him, but *he* had no intention of going away. He dropped down hard enough onto the couch at her left to bounce her skyward and topple the stack of financials that sat between them. The yellow paper-bound books—each eight inches wide, fourteen inches tall, and about a half-inch thick—slid sideways off the edge of her sundress and up against a board-shorted thigh.

He glanced down as he picked them up and stacked them in his lap, one at a time. His dark black hair was a tangled mess, smelling of both the warm sunshine and the salty sea breeze that had combed it into such disarray. The powerful, tanned bicep peeking out from beneath the sleeve of his yellow tee-shirt twitched from the slim effort. His head shook back and forth to let the light play with the slight shadow of afternoon razor stubble that covered his square jaw as he finished his task.

She tried her damnedest not to notice, just as she tried her damnedest not to notice the bright blue eyes that sparkled with mischief, or the smile that touched his lips when he glanced her way and caught her looking.

"These are prior year statements," he said, setting them down to his left. Holding out a hand, he added, "Gimme. The job doesn't start for two more days. Show me what's so important in that current report that you can't spare the time for even a little sunshine."

She didn't look away, but she ignored the request.

The bimbo, she reminded herself, fighting the charm of that simple smile and those endless eyes. *Remember the bimbo.*

His fingers found the report.

She didn't turn loose.

That damned cheating smile that he flashed her way wasn't special, even if it seemed to brighten the room far better than the setting sun. The little prick had already proven, beyond the shadow of a doubt, that he flashed it at anything that happened to wear a skirt; and the bigger the tits, the bigger the smile.

But he wouldn't let up. He started to pull—gently at first, but firmly. It soon became a struggle to keep the report tucked snugly in her lap. It was annoying, but she was *not* going to play tug-of-war with the arrogant little snot, even if her fingers ached to run across those broad shoulders, rustle through that tangle of hair, and stroke the cheek that would be warm and soft, yet so sand-papery rough.

"Thank you," he said when she let go. Then, glancing at the page she'd been trying to read for the last hour, he added, "Ah, I see. Investments. A lot of trading. A lot of *ins-and-outs* to these accounts, with very little progress at the end of the day. Not a very *satisfying* read, if you ask me. I'd stick with novels."

"Oh, grow up," she spat, rolling her eyes as she reached for the report.

"Nuh uh," he said, holding up his right hand as he dropped the report on top of the others to his left. "Not so fast. Walk first, report later. That was the deal."

"Deal? What are you talking about? There was no *deal.* Give that back."

She lunged. Laughing, he shielded the reports. She bumped into a very big, very powerful shoulder that burned beneath his shirt and smelled of coconut suntan lotion. Hopping up onto the couch, she reached across his back and down to the reports on the other side; but he'd already spirited them away and onto his lap.

They tussled for a moment, with her leaning right, then left—a bubbling laughter that she didn't quite understand suddenly coming from her own lips. She leaned left behind him again, stretching out with her fingers snaking around his long, lean torso to follow the reports, only to be batted away by a guarding left hand; but a quick tickle brought the elbow flashing back to his side and her fingers lunged forward to touch the reports in victory—

And then defeat as he leaned back, pinning her against the couch.

His shoulders burned into her chest, firing a heat bloom at the pit of her stomach that popped her eyes, sent a jolt upward to quicken her heart, and spread downward to warm parts of her body that she'd studiously ignored since the trip home. Steaming on the couch, but now for an entirely different reason, she froze—swept into a moment of whirling thoughts and spinning emotions.

But he was frozen, too.

He hadn't moved since pinning her to the couch, her breasts pressing deeply into his back. His weight held her just as tight, but a slight quiver rattled his frame from legs that seemed to be shaking. His forearm dropped onto her right hip, surprisingly light. His palm and fingers gently stroked her leg below the hem... but just once.

"I'm sorry," he said, his voice ragged and thick with emotion. "This was a bad idea. Now would be a good time for you to go."

He leaned forward a little, barely— grudgingly—giving her room to slide away while a low moan that was almost a pained growl quietly rumbled his ribs. She recognized the sound. It was the same one that she felt, the one that refused to let her move, even though she knew full well that she'd do something stupid if she stayed...

But what was wrong with that?

For an entire hour, she'd been wondering what was wrong with surrendering to a physical attraction if she recognized it for what it was. It wasn't love—it *couldn't* be love, since it was far too late for anything so whimsical to happen to Patricia Ann Foster—but the animal attraction, the pure, unadulterated *lust* that raced through her body and swept through her mind, refused to be denied.

Why fight it?

It was real. It was here. And for the moment, it felt so *right*.

Tomorrow would take care of itself.

Tonight was for her... one last time.

Eight

Patti came up from behind, arms stretched wide at the tips of his broad shoulders while drawing her chin up his spine. A shuddering tingle followed, rippling up his back in her wake. She moved slowly upward, taking her time until she found the back of his neck, then brushed over into the crook of his shoulder. He might have been a prick, but he was a damned sexy one. With her hot breath bathing his skin, she reached out to gently nip his lobe.

"No," she whispered.

Having made up her mind, she threw away all restraint. This was sex, pure and simple. Let the chips fall where they may; but at her whispered word he was once again moving, too. Turning his head, he found her mouth, his lips meeting her own. He kissed her, tentatively at first, then with more hunger and a need to match her own.

Reaching across his shoulder, he cupped the back of her head in the palm of his left hand. Pulling her close, he kissed her long and hard, even as his right hand stroked her leg deliciously soft, sending a tingle racing up her inner thigh to meet the burning fire that swept down from the pit of her stomach with dangerous results.

Oh, yeah.

To hell with right.

She'd take right now.

An hour later, or maybe it was only a few seconds, he broke away for one last try at a gallant chivalry that she never expected. "Last chance," he whispered softly, his deep blue eyes looking bravely into hers with a longing and a hurt that told her he was still willing to let her walk away, even now.

"Shut up and kiss me."

But he didn't kiss her.

Ducking his shoulder beneath her side, he rolled her down into the sunshine, cradling her within his warm, powerful arms—one behind her shoulders and the other sliding up beneath her dress at the knees. *Then* he kissed her, slow and lingering, before gently nipping her lower lip and moving off to nuzzle her neck. Eyes closing, she lifted her chin at his first electric touch, then tangled her fingers through his silky hair and turned her head, guiding his soft lips and rough chin to the sensitive spots behind her ear... beneath her lobe... down the curve of her chin... further south.

Either his lips were a miracle or she'd been away from the game too long. Patti purred at the attention, the satisfied growl low at the base of her throat refusing to go away; but just as before, she felt a rumbling echo deep within his chest.

The hand that had been softly stroking her thigh came away, taking a moment to smooth the dress down the outside of her leg before sliding up to cup the breast that his electric lips had finally found. His touch was tentative at first, waiting for her to shy away—and never mind the fact that her hands were tangled in his hair and guiding him wherever she damned well pleased—or perhaps he was afraid that he'd hurt her, or that she might break. It was sweet in a way, but the growing urgency between her thighs wished that he'd get things rolling.

Her nipples hardening beneath his touch, he squeezed and caressed with his powerful hands, nipped and explored with his questing lips, buried his chin deep in her cleavage at her command—but from the *outside* of her carefree little dress.

He refused catch a clue.

He wouldn't peel down the neckline.

It was low enough—and certainly something she could have shrugged out of if he gave her the chance—but his attention seemed focused on the same pattern, and the repeated pattern of his continued attentions were *really* starting to stoke the fires that he refused to quench.

The growls at the base of Patti's throat took on a note of frustration as her growing urgency caused her legs to squirm. Taking matters into her own hands—and why should this be any different from any other mountain that she'd ever moved—Patti put a palm on his chest and pushed him away.

"This isn't working," she said when he came up for air. Squirming out of his lap, she hopped onto the floor to stand in front of him, then turned and pulled her hair over her shoulder. Cocking her head, she looked back when he didn't move. It was all she could do to keep her voice light and cheerful instead of husky and horny. "Well? I'm waiting. Help me out of this, silly."

Without rising from his seat, he proved that his arms were as long as they were powerful. After a quick tug at the top of the dress, the shoulders loosened to the quiet sounds of a tiny nylon zipper. She thought about teasing. She told herself that it wasn't her burning need that made her stiffen her arms to drop the dress before he finished, leaving her standing in nothing but the skimpiest white panties she owned—and cursing a security agent with too much time on his hands and nothing to do. Instead, she convinced herself that with the blinding light pouring hot from the window, he wouldn't see a thing. It would have been a wasted show.

"Your turn," she told him, turning and dragging him to his feet.

He might have been surprised by the speed, but she didn't care. With her fingers under the hem of his shirt, she lifted, then stopped when the back caught and the shirt bound just above the six-pack of his tight abs. Crossing his arms, he reached down to help. She left him to his work, reaching instead for a hem of a different sort and pushing them down over his hips.

He might have pulled the shirt free, he might not. She didn't notice. He sprang free, big and bold and ready to play. Dropping to her knees, she rested one hand on the flesh at his hip and curled the other around his hard cock. It was thicker than she thought, burning hot. It was both soft to the touch, yet hard beneath her unyielding grip... something that she'd once known, but somehow forgot.

For long moments, she stroked his shaft as he stood with his hands resting gently at the back of her head, sometimes working her hand around the end to rub his swollen head with her palm, other times dropping her circled grip all the way to the tiny forest of curly hairs at the base of his shaft on the down stroke, then releasing her grip and rotating her hand to caress his balls and tickle the bottom of his shaft on the return.

He grew bigger from her increased attention, arching upward like some great beast waking from a long sleep. Her jaw ached as she caressed and played, and then she dropped her head, kissing him before guiding him deep inside.

He felt the shudder in his hip and the tightening of his fingers in his hair as she went down on him, claiming her prize. He'd been right about moments. This moment was too fine to ignore as she circled him with her tongue, sucking harder and deeper with every pull of her head. He continued to grow in her mouth, and still she didn't let up. Harder, deeper, and ever faster.

He groaned as his hips shook, an animal cry filled with the same frustration she'd felt only moments ago. His cock quivered deep inside her throat, but before he could find his release, he pulled her to her feet. Lifting her from the floor, he kissed her hard with a hunger like she'd never known. Wrapping her legs around his magnificent hips, she responded in kind.

And then he stumbled, losing his balance. Rocking back on his feet, he bumped against the couch and they went down, crashing onto the soft mattress. She landed in his lap with a sharp cry, his hands locked on her hips and her arms around her neck. He made an unnecessary apology as her own nervous laughter filled her ears.

"Have I ever told you that you rock my world?" he asked with a shy smile.

"You're the one with the rocks," she replied, arching an eyebrow. Repositioning her knees, she lifted herself up to capture him between her thighs. "Let's put 'em to good use." Before he could utter a word, she dropped down—slow and steady—driving his entire glorious length deep inside.

This time it wasn't a sharp cry that escaped her lips, but full-throated satisfaction—a satisfaction he echoed a moment later when she lifted herself up and rode him down again. She could scarcely believe what she was doing—or with whom she was doing it—but that was for another day. For now, as she began to ride him harder and faster, and as he moved to respond—cupping her breasts with his strong hands and dropping his mouth to nip her hardened nipples—she gave her mind a rest and plunged into the moment.

And a glorious moment it was.

As was the next...

And the one after that, too.

Nine

Hours later, long after the sun went down, Patricia Ann Foster reclined on the couch with her right hand tucked behind her head and the fingers of her left hand casually stroking the hair of the naked man asleep on her chest—a naked man lying on her left breast and breathing deeply enough, although not actually snoring, to send one blast of hot, lazy air after another rolling across her skin to keep her right nipple rough, aroused, and high in the sky.

She was still angry that the insensitive mass of bulging muscles had ruined her morning by flirting with a bimbo, but she reluctantly had to admit that she was pleased she'd made the right choice and hadn't let a ruined morning ruin the rest of her afternoon. The quiet voice that she'd assumed would ride her ragged about jumping the arrogant Mister Kirk Carter wasn't nearly as loud as she'd thought it might be, but perhaps that was due to thirty-plus-plus years of always listening to the damned thing. Or perhaps it was due to the fact that love was love, but she'd promised herself that this could only be lust. Or, maybe, it was because that quiet voice simply couldn't believe that she'd actually worn the younger man out.

Actually, Kirk wasn't so bad, although she'd never tell him... and then she chuckled quietly at her own little joke. He'd actually been quite *good,* once he relaxed and got into the swing of things. He'd left her tingling all over— enough so that she wasn't sure whether the pins-and-needles starting to shoot down her left leg were because of his skills or because the leg that he'd draped heavily over her thigh to rest between her own legs was cutting off her blood.

"What's so funny?" he mumbled, his deep voice rumbling through her chest.

"Oh, finally awake, are we?"

"I wasn't sleeping. I was enjoying the moment. You have the nicest breasts. Has anyone ever told you that?"

"Yes," she laughed softly. "They line up at the back door of my house every morning to tell me that as soon as I wake up. As long as you're not sleeping, though," she added, pushing on his chest, "get up. My leg's going to sleep."

He moved grudgingly, his warm cheek sticking to her skin as he peeled it away. Cold air washed across her chest, but the gasp that came to her lips was from the sudden pain of the blood flowing back into her leg, not the delicious tingle against her skin.

"Off," she said, pushing with more urgency, then sliding out from beneath his dead weight and hopping to her feet. "I've got a cramp. I've got to walk it off."

Padding softly across the floor on bare feet—with a generous limp—she opened the sliding door and stepped outside, closing it behind her as the night air added a brace of goose bumps to her tingling body. Leaning on the far railing, she stared out across a dark beach that was spread out beneath at least a million stars that winked brightly with every color of the rainbow.

The door whooshed open and closed behind her, as she'd expected. A moment later, the cool air at her back disappeared as his heat moved up behind her. He stood there, calm and quiet and not quite touching; but then something did brush her cheek—soft and gentle and smelling like a rose... mostly because it was.

"When did you get this," she said, taking the proffered flower as she glanced over her shoulder at the empty vase on the coffee table inside. "It's real. I thought it was fake."

"When did I get it?" he chuckled. "What do you mean? You gave me an hour. I picked up some bagels for breakfast, too, but I couldn't find any good luggage. All I found was the cheap stuff. We'll have to keep looking. What did you expect me to do with all that time?"

"I thought you'd be spending it with the blonde."

"What *blonde?*"

"The blonde! At lunch, remember? You kept looking over my shoulder at the blonde."

"No, I kept looking everywhere except your eyes. I was trying my damnedest not to tell you that you were getting screwed, but you were making it really hard. You were making my little friend hard, too. You do that a lot, you know. I still can't figure out how you managed to see him under the table, though. Care to share?"

"Oh... um... no," she told him, grateful for the darkness that hid the look of stunned comprehension that flashed across her face.

She'd been wrong about the blonde, all along. If she'd been wrong about that, what else had she been wrong about, and why was the quiet voice at the back of her mind suddenly so silent? She could practically feel it smirking away back there.

"It's one of those things," she added. "A girl can always tell, you know, so don't even think about getting any ideas when you see any *other* blondes lying around. I'll always notice."

"Yes, ma'am," he whispered at her ear, his big, strong arms wrapping her in a delicious heat that burst into a raging fire as he pulled her back into a warm embrace and began to nuzzle her neck. "Once she notices, though, any idea what she might plan to do about it?"

Wrapping her arms around his, she closed her eyes and smiled.

Too late for love?

Maybe, but then again... maybe not.

Perhaps dark and handsome wasn't such a fairytale, after all.

"If you're a good boy tonight, I'll tell you in the morning."

Made in the USA
Las Vegas, NV
28 April 2024